THE ULTIMATE
SCOOTER
GUIDE

They came gliding out of the mist. Eight figures riding state-of-the-art scooters.

And we just stood there — wide-eyed. Our jaws hung open as they started popping tricks, stunts, and moves like you wouldn't believe.

Mind-blowing grabs, truly rad grinds, totally incredible spins, twists, and plants . . .

Then they were gone.

And no one could say for sure if they had been real.

Except for me.

I knew.

Cuz I found the backpack.

It was stamped with the logo STREETSTYLERS, and inside was page after page after page of scribbled notes. Some in languages I still don't understand. Some with diagrams for tricks no human being could possibly do. Awesome stuff.

No one has seen the Streetstylers since.

It's time their skills were passed on . . .

THE ULTIMATE SCOOTER GUIDE

BEN SHARPE

Illustrated by Paul Cemmick

SCHOLASTIC INC.

New York   Toronto   London   Auckland   Sydney
Mexico City   New Delhi   Hong Kong

This one's for the three planks:
Dudley, Toilet Boy, & Corporate Kev
Cheese!

From The Chicken House:
Thank you Janet and Mandy!

ISBN 0-439-28554-2

All rights reserved. Published by Scholastic Inc., 555 Broadway,
New York, NY 10012, by arrangement with The Chicken House.

SCHOLASTIC and associated logos are trademarks and/or
registered trademarks of Scholastic Inc.

12 11 10 9 8 7 6 5 4 3 2 1   1 2 3 4 5 6/0 1

Printed in the U.S.A.
First Scholastic printing, February 2001

Contents

Your attention please!

Riding scooters is fun and exciting; riding them well requires practice and skill! Following the safety guidelines in this book may help minimize any injury, but the use of appropriate safety equipment is strongly recommended.

You've just gotten your hands on the ultimate guide to everything you could ever want to know about scooters. Whether you're:

◆ A total beginner looking to buy your first scooter.

◆ A push 'n' glide expert looking for some rad new tricks.

◆ Or, just wanting to find out more about the coolest, shiniest, urban-funkiest way to ride the streets . . .

. . . then you are definitely in the right place!

We are gonna guide you through everything from choosing your first scooter, to perfecting the kind of killer stunts and moves that'll get all your friends drooling.

So check out chapters one and two right now, and let's get down to some serious streetsurfing! ARRROOOOOOOOOOOOW!!!!

Before we leap on in, we need to be sure that we're all talking about the same kind of scooters here . . .

What the Streetstylers are not gonna talk about is motorized minipeds. Not to say they aren't cool. They most definitely are. It's just that they're the subject for another book. Besides, most of us aren't gonna be driving for a while, right? And we all know deep down that there ain't no power like push-power. Especially when it comes to seriously impressing your friends and being cool to the environment.

What we *are* talking is:
◆ **FOOT-PROPELLED**
◆ **SINGLE RIDER** (unless you're crazy enough to try piggy-backing!)
◆ **LIGHTWEIGHT SPEED AND TRICK MACHINES**
◆ **THE FASTEST AND GROOVIEST** way to get from A to B and to any other spots in between.

Why walk somewhere in ten minutes when you can *gliiiiiiiiiiiiiiiiiiiiide* there in three?! And look mega cool while you're doing it!

We *did* already tell you about the *cool factor*, right . . . ?

We didn't?

Well, take it from the Streetstylers – you *will* look sooooo cool. Oh boy . . . You WILL!

The Vibe

If you don't own a scooter yet, you've probably seen some around. If not, where have you been hiding? Scooters are the hottest craze of this fresh new century, and there's over a million streetsurfers out there just waiting for you to join them.

The Streetstylers still remember the first time one zipped past us. A bright metallic-silver blur, curving around corners and zipping through tricks. We were like, *HELLO!!*

Then the kid riding the scooter jumped off, folded it in one quick motion, and headed into school. That *totally* did it for us. We just had to get one! Well, how could we not be impressed with something that moved so fast and could still fold down small enough to fit into a school bag?!

So we bought one . . . and were totally *blown away*!

Cuz so much about these scooters is totally excellent.

Totally, totally excellent.

First Up

Scooting is super-easy to learn. It takes maybe fifteen minutes to come to grips with the basics of push, slide, and glide. You just need a tiny bit of brake control and a little natural balance. Sure, learning tricks and stuff takes a while longer, but the Streetstylers can promise you that after just one session you'll be asphalt-surfing like a pro. Especially if you follow our guidelines in chapter four!

Second Point

These scooters are truly light. Check the specs in chapter two, if you don't believe us. Even the heaviest are not much more than eight pounds. That means you can stuff one in your bag at school, the movies, wherever, and it won't break your arm off while you're carrying it. A double bonus, cuz you can grab a bus, train, or whatever and go scoot somewhere new without feeling like you're lugging a ton of metal.

Freedom!

Can you think of any other transport that gives you this much freedom . . . ? Neither can we. Try catching a bus with your mountain bike. Or ramming a skateboard in your bag and slipping into math class . . . It just ain't gonna happen.

You can use your scooter absolutely anywhere. On the sidewalks, on a track, off-road, or in the half-pipe. And you can have a whole load of fun whether you're with your friends, or just hanging on your own. Scooters are great for cruising, racing, or freestyle trickery. Especially when you've grabbed a few hours of practice without anyone else knowing. Not that anyone in the Streetstyler posse would be that sneaky . . .

Oh, wait.
We have to do the introductions.
These are the guys the
Streetstylers hang with, and
we thought it would help to have
them along on this book, cuz
they probably know some
stuff we don't . . .

Nah.

Well . . . maybe just a little.

name:
David Lions
age: 9

scooter type: none yet.
Don't know what to get.

likes: just want to ride.

specialist skills: none yet!!!

top tip: don't tell your mom
how much decent scooters
cost till you get to the shop.

name: Phantom Ollie
age: 13

scooter types: Micro Pro and Ciro.

likes: off-roading and cool tricks.

specialist skills: ollies and back-wheel jumps.

top tip: don't practice TailWhips indoors.

name: KT-90
age: 10

scooter type: Micro Classic.

likes: scooting around town with my friends.

specialist skills: curb bouncing. It is hard!!!!!!

top tip: stunts are for geeks!!!!

name: RikFly
age: 12

scooter types: Kickboard, and Razor MS 130 B.

likes: blowing your minds with serious moves and air!

specialist skills: everything.

top tip: watch me and learn!

name: Trinity
age: 11

scooter type: a Push-Ped.

likes: racing with my brothers.

specialist skills: I don't know!!!!

top tip: don't always kick with the same foot. You get less tired.

name: Chloe

age: 13

scooter type: Micro Air-Flex (and my brother's Xootr).

likes: skateparks.

specialist skills: grinds and wall-rides.

top tip: if you don't get a trick dialed right away, just keep on trying.

The Streetstylers know you will be in truly good hands listening to these guys. Especially when Chloe talks. That doesn't happen often, but when it does, you really want to pay attention. If there's a trick or stunt for any kind of scooter that Chloe can't do 100 percent perfectly, we haven't heard of it: She is one cool cat.

Not like Richard Flynn (aka RikFly). He's not half the rider he thinks he is. Thinks he can do a 360°TailWhip, but the Streetstylers ain't never even seen him complete a decent Ollie. You have been warned!

And if, after meeting geek-boy Rik, you need a little reassurance that scooters are as cool as the Streetstylers keep telling you, then check out how many MAJOR celebs we've bumped into while surfing those sidewalks . . .

Shine Like Stars

Jake Lloyd, Jon Bon Jovi, and sporty Mel C have all been seen with scooters. And extreme sports stars Eric Koston and Tony Hawk have both been checking out the possibilities for this rad new trick-discipline. Up for trying a 900° on one of these, Tony?!

The Streetstyler posse has also clocked Robbie Williams, Sarah Michelle Gellar, Alicia Silverstone, and those big rock dudes from Creed all getting down to some serious push 'n' glide action. No – not all together! Though can you imagine the race those guys would've had? Our money would definitely have been on those Creed boys –

did you see the moves they were pulling in their video?!

KT-90 spotted Mickey and Minnie scooting around Disney World.

We even hear rumors that Brian from Westlife has blown off his chauffeur, just cuz he can't get enough of asphalt-surfing!

But it's not just celebs who are bagging these scoots. The guys who developed *Toy Story 2* are famous for surfing around their offices on 'em, and loads of suity business-dudes have started push-powering to work. The Streetstylers are not too sure we would want to scoot in a suit (check out some better combos in chapter four!), but we respect them for at least trying to not be totally boring.

And . . .

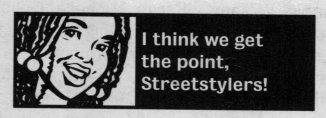

I think we get the point, Streetstylers!

Yeah. Who cares about celebs anyway!

Right. Er . . . All we were trying to tell you is that scooting is *definitely* hot. Fact.

And it's gonna keep getting bigger and bigger.

So, read right on, and let the Streetstylers help match you up with your ideal street machine!

There's Razors, Kickboards, Ninjas, Ciros, Xootrs, City Sticks, Push-Peds . . .

Whoaaaaaaaaaaa! Hold up!

No matter what anyone tries to tell you, buying your first scooter is really simple. Especially if you listen to the advice of the Streetstylers!

If you're a first-timer, you don't want to worry too much about add-ons and accessories. As long as you buy a decent brand, all the essentials you need to get street-surfing will be built-in.

> ### How do you know which brands are good?

Well!! Heh-heh-heh. Never let it be said that the Streetstylers like to dish dirt, *but* if a scooter doesn't have most of the stuff we talk about below, then it's a real **GLOPPER!**

Every good-quality ride should have this stuff. Minimum!

- ✘ A small, easily foldable frame.
- ✘ A telescopic steering column.
- ✘ An anti-slip deck-mat.
- ✘ A minimum of two wheels. (If yours has

less than two, some shop dude has sold you a unicycle. Not good.)

Strength!

Your scooter should also have a strong frame – either injection-molded aluminum (like the stuff they use to make jet planes) or a flexible wood-and-metal composite. That way, as long as you don't park it under a bus, it should stand up to almost anything you can put it through.

Weight!

The next thing you need to check out is weight. Scooters range from around six to eight pounds. If it's a heavy model, it should look a lot bigger – like the Xootr. If it's small and *still* heavy, then it's made from a bad material. Leave it! Always pick a scooter that feels comfortable to carry. You want to be floatiiiiin'!

Brake!

You need a good brake, too. If someone offers you a scoot without one, don't even think about it! A proper scooter will have either a molded rear-foot-brake, or a hand-brake. Either one is cool. The foot-brake may seem a little weird when you first try it, especially if you're used to riding a bike. But, after a few stuttering stops, you will have it dialed.

Safety!

Oh . . . One more thing before you buy. Ask what kind of safety checks your scooter has been put through. Top brands, like Razor, bash their test machines with all kinds of stuff before they approve them as safe. If your scoot has survived being beaten with a metal bar, it's a good bet it'll last through a lot of wipeouts on the street!!

And that's pretty much it . . .

 **So how come there are so many different brands?!**

A Little Bit of History

Way way back in 1996, you could only get two types of scooters – the Razor and the Micro. (And they were basically the same thing!). Then people started to want rides that could do a little more. Like go over bumps without knocking them off! Or grind curbs. Or speed over dirt. Or whatever.

So the two manufacturers started making different styles of scooters to meet all those different riders' needs. Pretty soon a whole load of other companies started making versions of the perfect street-machine, too.

Most scooters still look a lot like those early models. (All the Push-Peds, City Sticks, Ninjas, Zappys, as well as most of the Razors, JD Bugs, and Micros.) Well, hey – it was, and is, a design classic. And the Streetstylers know that lots of you will choose to buy one in that style cuz they are sooooo coooool. But, if you want something a little more specialized, here's a few of the really rad rides for you to check out . . .

The Micro Air-Flex

It may *look* like almost every other scoot, but peer a bit closer and you'll see some really hot stuff.

First up, it has a deck made of wood and glass-fiber. That's a more flexible combination than the usual aluminum type, so it can absorb a lot more jolts and bumps. It makes the scooter a little heavier at the base, too. And having a low center of gravity is not a bad thing when you're flying down a dirt track.

This baby also has air-filled tires, instead

of the usual resin, and ABEC-5 performance bearings. That means you get a nice smooth ride and a lot of wheel-turns per push.

But all those modifications would be useless if the deck-plate was low to the ground like on most other scooters. The good news? It's not. The ride position is set higher off the floor, so you won't have to avoid every last little stone or branch in your path. You can just scoot right on over them.

Streetstylers' spies say the brake is slightly better, too. That's got to be good news if you're giving it some serious off-road action and suddenly there's a tree stump right up ahead!

Here's the Micro Air-Flex's awesome vital stats:

frame:	aluminum
deck:	wood/glass fiber
handlebars:	aluminum
grips:	black foam
wheels:	black air-filled tires 5.9 in, 80 psi
brake:	rear (friction plate)
folded size:	27.9 in long x 9.3 in high x 13.6 in wide

total weight:	**8.6 lbs (varies between models)**
max. rider weight:	**221 lbs**

Had a wicked time with this. Went over bumps that would have totaled my old scooter!

It's OK, I guess, but only if you want to get dirty. I think my old Micro looks nicer!

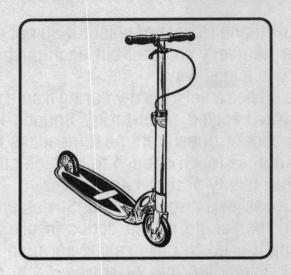

The Xootr

The first thing you need to know is that the "x" in "Xootr" is pronounced like the "z" in "zoo." The second important fact is that this scooter is BIG! Especially the ride-board. That's great news if you have huge feet, or like to wear big sneakers. You will be able to gliiiiiiide with both feet onboard, no problem. It's also cool if you're lazy. Having both feet on the deck means you can scoot longer distances without getting tired!

The Xootr has big wheels, too. They're about three times the size of normal skate-wheels, and made of ultra-glide polyurethane (a sort of plastic). So not only is the ride very smooth, but each push will take you a long way.

It also has a very hard-wearing frame and backward-angled front-forks. Sounds kind of science-y, doesn't it? All it means is that the Xootr is tough enough to bounce curbs and pull plenty of tricks and moves.

The design is awesome, too. Streetstylers heard that some of the dudes involved in making it used to build racing cars, so you will definitely get lots of stares if you ride one. Which is cool (unless you fall in a ditch . . . when someone you think is cute is watching . . . and the ditch is full of mud . . . Not that anything like that would ever happen to the Streetstylers).

Yeah, right!

There are three versions of the Xootr available, but they all come with the same basic stuff. Just give these figures an eyeballing:

frame:	aluminum
deck:	laminated-birch/aluminum /carbon fiber (varies between models)
handlebars:	steel
grips:	foam
wheels:	die-cast aluminum rims and polyurethane tires diameter 7.1 inches
brake:	rear (with hand lever)
folded size:	31 in long x 9.4 in high x 12.6 in wide
handlebar height:	adjustable to 38 in maximum
total weight:	9.9 – 10.6 lbs (varies between models)
max. rider weight:	251 lbs

I liked this a lot. The board is big and I could go pretty fast without falling off.

The handlebar brake is cool. All the scooters should have this.

Good wheels and bearings on this. I use my brother's when I want to get somewhere quick. A little heavy though!

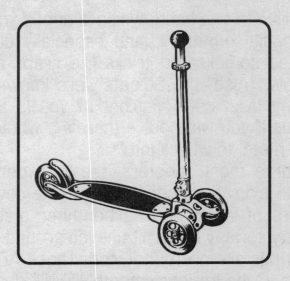

The K2 Kickboard

If you're thinking something a bit strange is going on here, then you're right.

The K2 has no handlebars!

Freaky.

Instead, you get a height-adjustable joystick with a bottom end that is fixed to the deck in a sort of knuckle-joint. Crazy, huh? Maybe. But it does mean you can bend the stick really low, making the K2 great for taking corners at speed. Smooooooooooooooth!

At the stick's *top* end, you get a flexible knob. This means you can steer the scooter easily with one hand, which is cool if you're carrying something, and especially cuz it makes complicated tricks like grabs a lot simpler. Also, the Streetstylers know that having less metal in front of you is a big bonus if you wipe out – there's a whole lot less metal to whack into!

Unlike most scooters, the K2's deck is made from a ply construction. The several layers of wood and carbon-fiber make it pretty springy if you hit uneven ground. The bearings are pretty hot, too. Those ABECs again. Good for long smooth gliiiiiiiiiiiides . . .

Kickboards also have an extra wheel at the front. Is this cool? Yep. If you're a nervous beginner, the K2 will give you a nice stable ride. And, if you're a pro, you can execute the tougher tricks more easily cuz you can really lean on this scooter. (It's much easier to concentrate on nailing a grind if you know the front end isn't just gonna slide away and land you on your tush!) The extra front wheel means the scooter stands up on its own, too. The Streetstylers love that. We can park it somewhere cool, step away, and milk those respectful glances. Oh yeah. Look. Admire. But NO touching.

Scope these vital vitals:

frame:	**aluminum**
deck:	**wood/glass fiber**
steering rod:	**aluminum**
wheels:	**clear polyurethane 3.9 in diameter**
brake:	**rear (friction plate)**
folded size:	**27.7 in long x 9.3 in high x 13.6 in wide**
total weight:	**7.1 lbs**
max. rider weight:	**220 lbs**

One **COOl-** looking scooter!

The pole thing is a little tricky.

You get some great suspension on this stick. Nice tough board and a real fast brake. Guess I'm saving up again...

Most of these scoots are available at your local toy or sports shop. Those that aren't can be bought on-line. In fact, the Streetstylers think that buying on the Net is the best way to pick up a good bargain. (Because they weigh so little, delivery costs are low, too.)

But don't forget... Cool new rides are being developed all the time. In fact, the Streetstylers heard that Ciro has just gone

one step further than the K2 people and has put four wheels on their machine. Funky.

If you **STILL** need more help deciding which scooter is the one for you, we have the answer . . .

Take the Streetstyler Urban Examination!

Just ask yourself this – are you:

A Speed Freak?

- You want to get where you're going as quick as you can.
- You're always looking for a steeper hill.
- You want to race your friends till the soles burn off your sneakers.

Streetstylers recommend . . .

Look for a light scooter and be sure to check for decent wheel-bearings. The better the bearing, the more turns you get per foot-push. That means it takes less energy to go farther, faster. After a little practice, you can get some serious speed.

The Streetstylers even heard rumors of hard-core racers getting speeds of close to 19 mph! (Though we're not so sure we believe that. Even 3 mph feels fast on a scoot!)

An Urban Joyrider?

- You're the cool kid around town.
- The scooter is just one part of your mega-hip look.
- You like to hang outside trendy shops, popping tricks and posing.
- You love the thrill of curb bouncing.

Streetstylers recommend . . .

All the top scooters look totally hot, so this comes down to which style you like the most. You can't go wrong with clean, silver lines. Metallic scoots look *extremely* cool when the sun catches them – just make sure you choose one with front suspension if you plan to do any serious trick-work. Or, if you really want to turn heads, the Xootrs and Ciros will definitely get people staring. Don't forget though, whatever scoot you get, there are accessories and individual tweaks you can buy or make to create a totally unique ride. Just check out chapter eight.

An Off-roader?

■ You like urban action, but love the thrill of dirt-riding.
■ You can't get enough of gliding between trees.
■ The tougher the terrain, the better the challenge.

Streetstylers recommend . . .

There's only one or two machines suited to this kind of scooting right now, but all the main suppliers say it's gonna be the next big thing, so you should have a lot more choices soon. An off-road scoot has to have a raised and flexible deck – to help you avoid those low-lying bumps and stones – plus decent suspension with air-filled tires to give a smoother ride. Don't even try off-roading any other way – your scooter and your body will be toast!

Trickster?

- No curb, wall, railing, or staircase is too much of a challenge.
- You're only happy pushing that scooter – and yourself! – right to the limit.
- Any day now, you really will perfect that 360° TailWhip.

Streetstylers recommend . . .

You can do basic tricks with all the scoots. And, if you are a real natural, you'll probably be able to coax out some fairly killer advanced moves, too. But, for really impressive-looking stunts, you're gonna need either a machine with a good bunch of add-ons – like a trick-bar and grind-plate, or a scooter-skateboard crossbreed, like the Kickboard, which is designed specially for trick-work.

Or do you just wanna hang out?
▪ And do a little bit of what you feel like!

Streetstylers recommend . . .
If you just want to ride and hang, any of the scoots will do the job. Our only advice is that you don't need to spend loads of cash on one of the newest models. The cheaper scooters are very cool. Just be sure you are buying from a decent supplier. Or, if you're getting one secondhand, make sure the seller is someone you trust!!

Because scooting is so trendy right now, some naughty companies have been making bad fakes of the decent brands. You may save a little cash getting a fake scooter, but you are not gonna be happy if it dismantles itself while you're cornering at speed! Streetstylers have seen that happen once too often.

**Get out there and grab
yourself an asphalt-
surfer, and we'll see you
again in chapter four!**

Listen up. You want to sound cool on the street, right? Then chomp onto the RikFly dictionary!

Air Any time you jump or Ollie, you are getting some air. Good scoot riders get big air!

Am This is some of you guys. It's short for amateur. If you practice real hard, you might get to be a pro like me!

Bail When you're in the air, and a trick has gone pear-shaped, you bail – leaping away from the scoot to try for a pain-free landing.

Bombing When you get some serious speed – usually down a big hill.

Burly A big trick with lots of potential for pain if you get it wrong! If you're a scoot rider who gets thrills from the trickier stunts, you're definitely a Burly.

Bust If you bust a trick, you've got it right! If you get busted, someone is chasing you off his land!

Carve Pulling off a big, fast, aerial scoot-turn.

Dialed When you get a trick right.

Dropping Good idea to shout this if you wipe out on a crowded skate ramp. "ARG!" works just as well though. . . .

Fakie A backward move – usually with just your rear wheel touching the ground.

Flatspots Clear spots on your wheels where the polyurethane has worn away during a trick.

Funbox Any sort of box – usually a wooden one – that you grind or slide on.

Glopper Someone who has made a really bad clothing decision. . . .

Gnarly When something's totally rad!

Goofy You're goofy-footed if you ride with your left foot at the back.

Grommet Little kid scoot-riders like David. Heh-heh-heh.

Hang Up Getting your front or rear wheel stuck during a trick. Better get ready to slam! (Also called a Lock.)

Hipper A huge, swollen bruise on the hip. You really *don't* want one of these!

Land To A successfully completed trick!

Mongo You are mongo-footed, or "pushing mongo," if you use your leading foot (the wrong one!) to push.

Mullet Really bad hairstyle. Also known as a Kentucky Waterfall, Hockey Hair, Tennessee Top Hat, Canadian Passport, Unhappy Peacock, or Ape Drape. (Hair that is left long in back and short in the front.)

HE-HE-HE-HE-HE-HE-HE!!!!!! That's you, Rik.

KT, I DON'T have a mullet!

Old Skool A trick, rider, or pretty much anything else that is old style.

Rad When something totally blows you away!

Ripper A good all-around scooter-rider

Session Any time you get together to scoot with your friends.

Sick When something's totally gnarly!

Sack It If you bail and land with something smashed up between your legs – usually your scooter's steering column – then you've sacked it.

Sketchy Someone who's a little bit weird . . . and probably a glopper.

Slam A VERY hard fall.

Snake Someone who cuts you up bad, or steals your line into a trick.

Swellbow The grisly result of falling on your elbow!

Technical (Or Tech) Any trick performed on flat ground or a fairly low ledge, involving plenty of technical skill, such as a 360° TailWhip.

Tech Dog A scoot-rider who is really hot at technical tricks.

Tweak Adding a personal touch to a well-known trick.

Bet you never expected to learn a whole new language, huh? And the cool thing is, folks are making up new phrases all the time, so there's nothing stopping you from adding your own faves.

Hey dudes! Got your scoots now? **Cool!** Let's **RIDE!**

Whooooaaaaaaa! Easy tiger! Before you hit the streets you need to get the Street-stylers' lowdown on scooting safety.

Oh brother!

Rik, dude, you were in the hospital TWO WEEKS that time you didn't wear your helmet!

Er... OK. Maybe safety is important...

Safety is NOT a dirty word. Take it from the Streetstylers. We've seen the scars.

All the scooter-makers recommend you wear a helmet and pads, even if you're just gonna be scooting around your yard, and the Streetstylers are totally with them on that. There is no way you would be allowed to do your stuff in a skate park without protection, and riding on the sidewalk ain't no different.

I know what you're thinking though. Am I still gonna look cool on my scooter if I'm wearing crash-protection gear?

Want the simple answer? YES! You will. And this is why:

The top scooter riders, skaters, and in-line skaters are all sponsored by big sports companies. They don't want their riders to look like they've gone one-on-one with a gorilla, so they've developed all kinds of trendy-looking safety gear. You can get some truly rad stuff to protect every single part of your body from a mashing. Most of it is color and style-coordinated, too. You really don't have to look like your head got stuck inside a bowling ball to be safe.

Heads Up!

Stuff your head in a quality helmet. There are loads of good brands out there. Razor makes helmets especially for scooter riders. Boeri, Roces, and Logic are all worth checking out. Basically anything that meets your country's safety standards is cool.

Pro-Tek-Shun!

Wrist guards are a good idea, too. Most times when you fall, your hands automatically shoot out to try to soften the impact. Wearing guards means you are less likely to sprain or snap a wrist. YeooooOOW! If you plan on doing some of the advanced tricks we show you later in this book, we seriously recommend you look at getting some knee and elbow guards. Smashing up either of those joints is a REALLY BAD IDEA!!!

What the Streetstylers really can't figure out is why anyone *wouldn't* want to wear safeties. Scooting can be a dangerous enough sport anyway. Everyone we know has all the right gear, and they still carry the scars of sidewalk conflict!

Da Boneyard

My worst? We were doing stair jumps down at the Square. The scoot just flew right out from under me as I landed. Scraped all the skin off my knee, ripped my pants, and dislocated my little finger. That really hurt!

Scratched arm and bruised thumb.

Doing X-Ups at Playstation Park – I went to grab some Cokes, tripped, and broke my wrist!

Two black eyes, a chipped tooth, a broken nose, a squashed ear, bruises all down my left side, and my clothes torn to pieces.

Wasn't that when your little sister beat you up, Rik?

KT – you're so NOT FUNNY!

Hmmm . . . If you want to keep scrapes to a minimum, the Streetstylers' six hints for keeping body and scooter together will help:

One Always check over your scooter before you ride it. Make sure all its quick-release switches are in the locked position. Scope out whether any screws or levers have worked loose. Give each of the wheels a good spin to make sure they are all turning freely – and that none of them have gotten too worn.

One time I forgot to check my handlebars. I pulled an Ollie and the column shot right out of the deck-plate. Was mostly embarrassing, but could have hurt a lot . . .

Check your safety gear, too. If your helmet got damaged last time out, or your pads were torn, get new ones.

And don't trap your fingers when you fold or unfold a scooter. It really hurts!

Two Car drivers are your enemy! They never look carefully when they are on the road so you have to do the watching for them. Don't go zipping into a road, or out of your driveway without checking first. The Streetstylers are too young to be going to funerals!

Some kid on my street used to scoot in the road. He got run over and nearly died.

 # !!! STAY OFF THE ROAD!!!

Three Don't ride your scooter in any dumb places. There are loads of paved areas and skate parks around, so you really can stay clear of roads. Also, if you're planning to do tricks, make sure you do them somewhere where you have a good view all around. Doing a stair-jump and totaling your teacher is not too wise.

I only got suspended for a week....

 And then your Mom grounded your butt for three months!

Four Watch out for bad weather conditions. Scooters aren't designed for wet ground so you need to take things really slowly and keep your foot over that brake. And don't even think about riding on icy or oily surfaces!

Five Don't ride your scooter at night unless you've *covered* it in reflective strips and you're wearing reflective clothing. Scoots don't show up anywhere near as well as bikes, so you need to look extra-extra-visible.

And chill! You can STILL look cool. Bright orange and yellow jackets are soooo in. Or you could get some flashing beads for your hair. Well . . . maybe not if you are a guy. Unless you have mullet–hair like Rik!

Six Know your limits. If you haven't mastered an Ollie, don't try anything crazy like a Tail-Whip. You need to be able to control the scoot in your sleep first!

And if you ever get into trouble pulling a stunt – jump off! Better to bail while you still can. A few sidewalk scrapes are way better than a full-frontal hug from a brick wall.

Now . . . Let's surf those streets!!! AROOOOOOOOOOOOW!

There is no big trick to riding a scooter. Everyone's style is a little different and it'll take you a few tries to figure out what's most comfortable for you. The Street-stylers' top tip is to start out somewhere quiet. Find a stretch of sidewalk that is flat and straight – and isn't already full of pro riders! And take it SLOW.

Standin'

When you first get on the scooter, place your standing foot (the one you won't be kicking with) at a slight angle near the front of the deck. That'll leave room for the toes of your kicking foot to rest just behind it in between kicks. It also means the heel of your kicking foot will be hovering lightly over the rear brake (if your scooter has one) ready for use.

Kickin'

OK. Now you're ready to ride. Plant your kicking foot on the sidewalk and try for a strong and fluid kick. Looking cool on your scoot is all about gliding, not stamping at the ground in an energy-sapping frenzy. Who wants their friends to see them red-faced and stinky with sweat-patches? Not the Streetstylers. Take it from us: Steady, rhythmic kicks are the way to go. And remember to change feet regularly, too. Otherwise you'll end up with one leg twice the size of the other!

Plantin'

If you get tired quickly it's cuz you're working muscles that don't normally get used a lot. After a couple of days you should start to feel OK. If not, you need to make sure you aren't riding like a dork!

To scoot a long way and still be full of energy, you need to be planting your kicking foot down toward the front of the scooter. That way you propel yourself and the machine forward. Your kicking foot should always hit the ground close to the scoot, too. If you plant too far away, you'll just unbalance yourself, and end up with a way wobbly ride.

Don't bend your knees too much either. It's another way to waste energy. So is putting too much weight on your kicking foot. Spread your weight across the deck if you want to keep an even balance the whole time you're onboard.

Curbin'

Once you've got kicking under control, try getting up and down curbs without slowing down (or falling off!). This move is all about timing. Glide up to the curb and, just as you are about to touch it, put your foot down ready to push. At the same time, lift up your front wheel so that it's resting on top of the curb. And *push*. Simple.

Cornerin'

Now all you need to learn is how to turn. When you're gliding around slowly, this is easy – you just move the handlebars! But when you're really zipping along, you've gotta be a little more sly. As you turn your scoot into the corner, bend toward the handlebars and shift your weight outward so that your body leans into the curve. You don't need to lean much, unless it's a massive corner. Just do enough to stay balanced, and keep some pressure on the brake, too. You don't want your scooter's back end to slide away and spin you into a HUGE wipeout! If your scooter does start to slide, either jam on the brake and skid to a halt or . . . BAIL OUT! If you *have* to bail, remember to run off the scoot. If you just leap off and try to stand still, your momentum will have you kissing that sidewalk. Nasty!

And that's basically all the skills you need for hanging out, or cruising in town. But to do more advanced scooting, you need a bit more savvy . . .

SpeedFreakery

To be a genuine and bona fide white-knuckle rider is easy. You just gotta go fast, and finish first! For that, all you really need is good rhythm and a strong kicking action. It's also cool if you can find a pretty steep hill to help build up your speed. If you're racing with your friends, the Streetstylers think you should put most of your effort into making a quick start – like a sprinter does. Then settle down into a steady push and gliiiiide. If you don't get in front from the start, try for a burst of speed as you approach a corner. That way you can cut across the scooter ahead of you and make him chew your dust! But *no* pushing or jostling! Scooter riding is NOT a contact sport!!

Remember how you need to lean to get around a corner at speed? If you're a SpeedFreak, you want to get really good at doing this. You want to be a cornering *master*. Some of the best speed-riders lean so far out from their scooters and crouch down so low that they actually have to balance one hand on the road to steady themselves! If you get *that* good, go buy yourself some hard-wearing gloves!

There are two wickedly fast and freaky games you should try out if speed is your bag: Circuits and Road Raging.

Circuits

Find a big, flat expanse of concrete. Somewhere like a deserted parking lot. Mark out a course with your bags, coats, chalk, and even street cones if you can find any. The more stuff you can use, the groovier your circuit will look.

A good course will be sort of circular, like a racetrack, so there're plenty of good corners. You should try to find somewhere that is slightly sloped, too. That way you will have a downhill section where you can really FLY and an uphill section where you have to push like crazy! Then all you do is decide the number of laps you're gonna race and go! go! GO!

You can race your friends head on in a massive free-for-all, go one-on-one, or take it in turns doing time trials against the clock. It's all totally addictive! If your posse all scoots at about the same speed, you can add stuff to the circuit to make it trickier. Try laying a plank of wood across the straight to Ollie over, or putting up a mini-ramp. (You'll learn the skills you need to perfect these moves in the tricks section.)

Road Raging
This can be a real hoot. And it's simple cuz you don't need any equipment. It's just you, your friends, and the sidewalks where you live.

All you do is decide where you're gonna race to and what route you're gonna take to get there. The race should last at least a few blocks, and you should try to include as much crazy stuff as possible – like making everyone run up a steep bank, or down some steps (you could try an Ollie there if you are feeling really brave!), or over gravelly ground . . . you get the picture. Just use your imagination and try to come up with the trickiest, hairiest course possible. And as soon as you all complete it, challenge yourselves to do it in reverse!

Off-roading

Gliding off-road is like no other kind of scooting. You're gonna encounter all sorts of crazy stuff that you would never meet on the sidewalk. Branches are gonna whip out at you, vines and roots are gonna try to snag your wheels, mud is gonna clog your brakes, and birds and rodents are gonna fling stuff at you. It's a dirty world – and the Streetstylers LOVE it!!!

But before you head for the hills, there are a couple of things you really need to know.

One Off-road scooters are not total all-terrain-vehicles. You can't ride through thick mud or piles of heavy leaves. The wheels are just too small. What you can do is ride over gravel, wood chips, and pretty much any kind of dry earth, so long as it's not *totally* blitzed with holes.

Two To off-road well, you need to have excellent balance, top braking skills, seriously good slide-control, and lightning reflexes to make sure you stay on that deck! This is cuz your scoot will squirm around loads on loose ground.

The trick is to counterbalance.
If your scooter flips to the left, lean to the right. If it squirts out to the right, lean the other way. Sometimes this won't straighten out the scooter's front end, but it's better to slide sideways than to eat earth!!!

Three The first few times you try off-roading, you're gonna get *really* dirty. The Streetstylers must've fallen off at least twenty times on our first visit to the forest! If you stop regularly and clean all the gunk off your wheels – especially the back one – you won't spill so often. If you don't clean it, the back wheel can get clogged and stick to the brake. This usually happens at the worst possible moment, and when you least expect it! The scoot's back end will drag, or lift, and you'll be collecting your arms and legs from a bush. So clean those wheels!

Circuit racing is a little hard off-road – and also less fun, cuz it's hard to get the speed you need. But you'll be getting enough thrills from dodging obstacles and making that dirt fly! You *can* Mud Rage though. The rules are the same as for Road Raging, you just get a heck of a lot muddier, and you can dream up even crazier stunts! Come up with a route that includes grinds against logs, or a tree climb, or fence-jumping, or stream-wading, or . . . Well, you get where we're coming from!!

Oh ... One last thing. If you are going off-roading somewhere on your own or with friends – tell someone where you're gonna be. The Streetstylers are too busy to organize search parties!

Trickster

If you're a trick-head, we have some great news – you get three whole sections of rad stunts to try out later in the book! But first we want to talk about Horse. This is a cool game to play if you're hanging with a group of friends. And it's simple, too – as long as you can do some tricks!

The game starts with one of your posse popping a trick. Then everyone else has a crack at it. Anyone who fails the trick takes the letter "H." Then the next person pops a stunt, and those who can't copy it take an "H," if they did the first stunt, or an "O" if they messed up on the first go round. The winner is the last person in the game not to have spelled out the word Horse. We guess you could use any word if you liked, but for the Streetstyler posse, it's just always been "Horse."

Until now you've been scooting some-where nice and quiet, where no one could see you. Now you're ready to go public and hit the streets for real. So you're gonna want to look cool, right? No sweat. Just heed the advice of our resident fashion queen, KT-90. By the time she's through with you, you are gonna look great!

OK , people. I may not know a lot about tricks. But when it comes to being cool, you better listen up!

Hey! How about me . . . I got a lot to say about clothes and stuff!

Rik, your mullet does the talking for you. Beat it!

Names

Before you think about what clothes to wear, you should come up with a riding name. Mine's KT-90 cuz my name is Katie Morris and I was born in 1990. Cool, huh? If you hang with a group of friends, it's good to have similar nicknames to show that you're all part of the same scooter posse. I mostly scoot with my friends Joseph Kobi (Kobes) and Evelyn Ashton (EV-89). And we are the K Kollective cuz of our names and cuz we live on Kingston Road.

Your nickname doesn't have to have anything to do with who you are or where you live though. There're these riders called Mingus, Planet, and Prince W. They figure they are the Deck DJs cuz they like music, but we call them the Posh Posse cuz they all come from big houses and always wear designer labels!

If you can't think of a groovy name for yourself or for your scoot gang, try picking a couple of words from the list below.

CRAZY	RAD	LO
METHOD	DEMON	PLANT
QT	POW	CAT
FIVE-OH	BOMBER	GHOST
PRO	SLAM	SPEED
RAZOR	MONKEY	GIRL
BOY	SILVER	SMOKE
STREET	AIR	ANGEL
DAWG	BEANY	MAGIC
ASPHALT	STAR	FREAK
SURF	TRICKSTER	DIRT
WARRIOR	GLIDER	DUDE

Stick some cool ones together and KT-90 will guarantee you the hippest names in town!

Thinking about the sort of stuff your posse likes to do will help as well. A name like Da Dirt Demons is great if you're off-road freaks like Phantom Ollie and his crowd. But it just makes you sound like gloppers if you're Urban Joyriders. If you hang in town, you need a sleeker name like Silver Gliders or Urban AllStarZ.

Gear

It can be pretty embarrassing if you get caught wearing the wrong kind of outfit for the wrong kind of scooting. But imagine if you wear the wrong sort of clothes altogether . . . Eek! If you want to escape shame on a MAJOR scale, avoid this stuff like the plague:

Skin-tight Cords Just tragic.

Hand-knit Sweaters Thanks Gran, but money will be just fine next year.

Platform Shoes Try it. I did. Then I bought a new pair of shoes.

Mullet Hair You mean you've seen Rik and still need a reason?!

Trench Coats A one-way ticket to over-heating.

Loose-hanging Jewelry Looks great till you hang it around the handlebars . . .

Flip-flops It's sad, but these are just TOO hard to ride anything in!!

And you know if I catch you wearing ANY of that stuff I'm just gonna have to scoot off in the opposite direction!! So do yourselves a favor and follow *these* freaky fashion and lifestyle hints!

UrbanJoyriders

Fashion queen KT always says that there are two things you should never leave home without: rubber-soled shoes and a mini-backpack. Rubber soles, like on my Nikes, help keep your feet on the scooter's deck, and the bag means you can take a drink with you (Urban Joyriders *always* drink water. Soda is for geeks!).

For clothes, you should head downtown or to the mall. As long as what you buy is light and trendy, you will gain max respect.

For sounds, your radio just *has* to be playing some blissed out urban noise. From the ultra-cool soul of Macy Gray to the huge sprawling sounds of Radiohead and Travis, your choice of music should be as smooooooooooth as your style of scooting!

SpeedFreaks

Trinity says that part of *being* quick on her scooter is *feeling* quick. Well, she definitely looks speedy to me. I never see her in anything that's not tight, shiny, and just a little bit funky. She gets most of her clothes in sports shops, and is a real fiend for Reebok, Speedo, and Adidas. Her brothers all wear shorts, backpacks, and sports T-shirts — oh, and of course, pads and helmets. They all have sunglasses, too. When you're riding fast, it's the only way to stop an eyeful of dirt.

The main thing SpeedFreaks have in common with us Joyriders is footwear. If you're gonna be road racing on your scoot, you just have to wear lightweight sneakers. Trin has a pair of sneakers that I'm so jealous of!! She also has a very cool Storm wristwatch with a timer. It totally matches the color of her scoot and is something she just couldn't do without — it's the only thing that stops her brothers from cheating!

And what's Trin's soundtrack for whupping those boys' butts? Speedfreaks love any sound with pace and power!

Off-roaders

Why anyone would want to get all dirty scooting off-road, I just have no clue. But if you *do*, then normal scoot-gear just won't cut it. You need heavy-duty clothes to protect you from branches, rocks, and brambles – and to save your skin when you wipe out on that gravelly terrain!! Synthetics or thick-woven denims are the ONLY way to go – and it helps if they're waterproof, too. You can pick up some good brands in sports shops. Or you could try some specialized skate and scoot-wear. Most of their products will be breathable, water-resistant, and hardwearing.

You'll also need very sturdy footwear. You could probably get away with running shoes on a really dry day, but if you trail your push-foot along the ground to help with cornering, the sole will soon get worn down. Bad news! Instead, go for some kind of hard-soled boots. And don't forget those shades. I don't want anyone crying when they get grit in their eyes!!

Tricksters

You will definitely need hard-wearing gear for doing stunts! Chloe is forever having to buy new T-shirts after she gets shredded.

She usually goes for thick, baggy hooded sweatshirts, pants, and says there's no point spending loads of money on them cuz they get wrecked so quickly – especially when your'e trying tricks for the first time. Plus, baggy gear means you can keep your pads on all the time, without getting weird looks on the bus, or wherever.

If it's hot, then you have to wear a vest-top or T-shirt and knee-length shorts. It's the rules! And the crazier the logo, the greater the respect! But by far the most important thing is the shoes you choose.

You need something strong and flexible, with lots of grip and protective strips. The cool thing is that skateboard shoes are great for scooter riders, and there are hundreds of excellent brands making those! Don't buy 'em unless they give you *maximum* comfort!!

Trickster music is all about bringin' da noize!!! Chloe is into some really far out stuff, from The Beastie Boys to the old-skool sounds of the Red Hot Chili Peppers.

Rik listens to bad music — but we all knew he was a dweeb anyway!

Chill out, Rik. Some of your music's cool. And KT's, too. It'd be a real downer if everyone liked the same stuff. No one has to dress a certain way, either. Being different is cool. One time we dressed in boiler suits and big furry wigs and scooted around my neighborhood. It was a total hoot!

No more messing around. Coming at you now is the first of the Streetstylers' quick-fire guides to all the top tricks and totally rad stunts on the PLANET. So grab your scooter and your safeties, strip off that backpack, and prepare for some hard-core asphalt action!

The Ollie

You need to have this skill in the bag if you want to do a whole load of the more advanced scooter moves. The Ollie is *the* best way to get some air without the aid of curbs, steps, or specially designed ramps. And if you can get air, you can jump your scooter onto, over, and off just about anything. So if you were wondering which trick to learn first, this is most definitely the one!

You should try practicing it on the spot to begin with. Then, as you start to get more height, you can give it a try in motion. Each time you get it right, you'll go a little higher. After a while, the only thing keeping you on Earth will be the trick rider's arch enemy – gravity!

Do The Trick

Start off by carefully positioning your feet. Your back foot should be near the back of the deck, with the heel raised and your weight centered on the ball and toes. Your front foot should be near the head of the scoot, and angled forward.

Make sure you are comfortable with the balance, then push down with your back foot. Right away jump up, leading with your back foot and follow with your front foot after sliding it right to the front of the deck. (This probably sounds

complicated, but it's just about working out the timing. Once you get that figured out, you WILL be hooked!)

When you jump, pull the handlebars with you, that way you'll gain more height. Then, while you're in the air, bend your legs and relax your arms. Doing this helps to cushion your body so it's ready to absorb the landing.

And that's it! You've completed your first scooter trick. The only extra thing you have to learn, if you want to pull off the perfect Ollie mid-glide, is how to land and continue scooting smoothly. Once you've got that sorted out, you can start using the Ollie to clear obstacles or jump curbs and steps. And there's only one way to get that dialed: Lots of practice . . . and probably a bruised butt!

Ollie Manual

Want to do wheelies on your scoot? Then you're gonna love this!

The Ollie Manual is the next step up from a basic Ollie. It looks great and will help you develop balance and control over your scooter when doing stunts.

Do The Trick

To pull off the Ollie Manual, you need to be cruising at a good speed, so set yourself scooting with some strong, firm kicks. Then, do a normal Ollie, but try to land on the back wheel only. Pull on the handlebars to keep the front of the scoot in the air and wheelie down the sidewalk as far as you can before grounding it. Woooooo-Hooooooo!

Three things will help you get it right:

+ Positioning your feet so you can balance over the back wheel (but without pressing on the brake).

+ Arcing your body forward toward the handlebars.

+ Keeping the handlebars raised as high as you comfortably can off the ground. (Not easy, but so, so rad when you get it dialed!)

One way to get good at this trick is to chalk some marks on the ground and challenge yourself to wheelie that distance. Don't give up till you can do it several times in a row. You really want to be hot at this. The Streetstylers want you to be able to Ollie Manual in your *sleep*! Getting it nailed will make loads of the complicated tricks a whole lot easier.

 If you want to use the Ollie Manual to jump a curb, a top tip is to not Ollie too high. You want your scoot's back end to be just high enough to clear the curb. That way you can slam the rear wheel down right away and begin wheelie-ing while you still have lots of speed. (The slower you are moving, the harder it will be to balance.)

180°

After Ollies, this is definitely the next most useful trick to have under your belt. It's also the best and coolest-looking way to change direction while you're scooting. You do it by Ollie-ing and using your body weight to spin the scooter around in the air. The idea is to end up facing the opposite way to where you started.

Like most of the tricks, it's a lot harder than it sounds, and a lot of people have real problems getting enough turn on their jumps. If you only manage a 45° to start with, don't worry, you are still looking good! And remember that the more you twist your body, the more momentum you will get.

Do The Trick

Bend your legs into the Ollie position and jump as high as you can. As soon as you take off, turn your shoulders and upper body to the left or the right. (The Streetstylers recommend turning to the right if you are right-handed and to the left if you are left-handed.) As long as you keep a really tight grip on the handlebars, the scoot should turn and spin with you through the air. As you land, bend and relax your body like you would to complete a normal Ollie.

It will take you a while to learn how far to

turn your shoulders. To begin with, your turns will probably be too little or too big. With practice, knowing how far to twist your body will start to come naturally, and you will have learned one of the most useful stunts of all.

BunnyHop

Ever watched trail biking? Those riders do this stunt a lot, and it's pretty simple as long as your sense of balance is OK. It's a bit like doing an Ollie Manual, except you start from a standing position, and "hop" without the back wheel turning (instead of letting it glide you along).

Do The Trick

All you have to do is slide both feet toward the rear of the scoot, so that your right foot is over the brake and your weight is balanced over the back wheel. Then you pull up the handlebar to a 45° angle, and "hop" the scoot along by jumping and landing on the back wheel.

It's not the *most* impressive trick in the world, but it's great for jumping your scoot up curbs, or over cracks in the sidewalk. And it starts to look very cool if you use it as part of larger trick routines, or do something a little different with it. Try doing a series of hops – or even backward hops – if you want to grab some attention.

TailTwitch

This trick gives you pretty much the same results as an Ollie. The only difference is that you get to show off more!

Imagine there is an obstacle on the sidewalk and you're scooting straight at it. You could leap off your scooter, or whiz around the outside. But wouldn't it be cool to make like you were gonna Ollie over it, then, at the last second – while you're airborne – push the scoot's tail out to 45° and bring it back again before you land! The Streetstylers can already see the jaws dropping on your friends! Oh YEAH!

The key to bagging this move is being shifty quick with your footwork and keeping your back foot against the brake so that the deck can't get away from you. You could practice with an imaginary obstacle to begin with – otherwise you'll just keep spilling!

Do The Trick

First up, you need to get enough speed going to complete the move. As you get close to your "target," push back your rear foot so that it's to the back of the deck and squashed over the foot-brake. Then Ollie, and bring the leg that's on the brake forward and to the right. Your momentum will shoot the deck out to the right, too. Then, as you come back to earth, slide your foot back to its original position – your feet and the deck are facing forward. When you land, either ease off the brake to continue scooting, or keep it hammered down to make a sliding stop.

Try combining it with an Ollie Manual land- ing if you're feeling *really* cocky!

CurbRide

This move's a real crowd-pleaser when you're cruising the streets. And it's one of those tricks where you'll be glad you learned the Ollie and the 180°.

The idea is to jump onto a curb, planting the scoot's nose and front wheel over the edge, then jump back off while spinning to perform a 180°, so you land facing away from the curb.

It's best to practice this one on a low curb to start with – one that you can Ollie quite easily.

Do The Trick

Cruise on up to it, then Ollie so that you land facing the sidewalk, with half the deck on the curb and half off. Be sure to have your weight slightly toward the front of the scoot – otherwise you will ground the deck and either slide off, or be totally unable to do the second part of the trick.

Next up, Ollie back off the curb, twisting your body as you would for a normal 180°.

Hopefully you will land facing away from the curb and ready to ride off into the arms of your adoring fans!

Like a lot of the tricks, you can do a bunch of variations with this move. One cool option is to twist further and go for a 270° (a three-quarter turn). That way you will land right alongside the side-walk, which looks real smooth. It's very easy to have a BIG, messy spill practicing this though! So the Streetstylers recommend that you be very careful. And *never* forget to wear your safety gear. Not ever.

Learning these moves will give you plenty of ammunition to impress your friends. Not only that, they're a totally excellent launch-pad into the world of really complex scoot trickery. But before you get to that, have some of this . . .

Before you try out the next batch of awesomely complicated tricks and stunts, take a breather and check out Phantom Ollie's lowdown on personalizing and modifying your scoot. They will totally inspire you to grab some huge air!

Hi guys. The Streetstylers have asked me to talk to you about making your scooter look a little different. I guess because I have a pretty rad one. It's based on my favorite movie. *The Phantom Menace.* That's how I got my nickname, too.

Modifying your scooter is easy and a lot of fun. You can cover the frame in stickers, or paint designs on it. You can even bolt on some specially made accessories that the scooter manufacturers and designers have started making.

Handle-grips

One of the simplest things to change is the handle-grips. Most scooters come with black grips that you can pull off easily, and swap for all sorts of rad colors – like blues, reds, and crazy fluorescents. I even saw one girl with brown furry ones! She probably made those herself though. All you would need is some fabric, scissors, and strong glue.

Deck-grips

The deck-grip is simple to replace, too. Your scoot normally comes with the company's logo as a deck-grip. These look pretty cool, but if you want something unique, you can quickly peel and scrub it off with warm, soapy water. I got a special *Phantom Menace* grip on-line, and there's all kinds of other crazy stuff around, like leopard prints or zebra stripes. If you're going to make your own, just remember to choose something with a nonslip surface – the deck-grip is supposed to help you stay on the scooter!

Wheels

The wheels are designed to be replaced easily. That's cuz they wear out if you scoot a lot. New ones come in all different colors. I have one blue and one fluoro-orange, but you can get pretty much any combination. Having different colors looks cool when you go fast.

LEDs

But not as cool as fitting LEDs! These are some of the gnarliest add-ons you can buy for a scoot. LEDs are little red lights that snap onto your deck-plate and are completely motion-sensitive. That means they only flash when you are in action. And they look totally rad when you're doing tricks! You can get light-up wheels, too, but they aren't so cool, cuz they cost more than normal ones and you still have to replace them just as often.

Bearings

Another easy thing to change is your scoot's wheel bearings. Your machine will most likely come with fairly standard ones, so if you upgrade, you'll get a noticeably smoother and slightly faster ride. Bearings are rated on smoothness using a measurement called ABEC. The smoother a bearing is, the better it will work. The best bearings are ABEC 7. The worst are ABEC 1. Anything over ABEC 3 is cool for scooters, but if you want to race or do tricks, go for something a little higher. You can buy kits that include a set of ABEC 5s, spacers (to keep the bearings at an equal distance), and an Allen wrench to fit them. If you're not sure about fitting them yourself, someone in a skate shop should be able to help.

You'll probably need some shop hints for a few other upgrades, too. One popular one is to fix a BMX-style hand-brake to the handlebars. You definitely get improved stopping power with one of these, but it's hard to fit it yourself without leaving the brake-cable flapping around – especially when you try to fold the scoot. This can be a little dangerous cuz you could get caught up in it when you wipe out. So get some help.

Steering Columns

It's also possible to change your steering column for one that ends with a suspended front-wheel fork – very cool for tricksters, and I've even seen some scooters where the single wheel at the front or back has been replaced with a set of two in-line-style ones! It looks cool, and will definitely improve speed and balance, but it's probably not an adjustment to try yourself. Oll's advice? Seek professional help!

Grind-plates

One add-on you can fit yourself is a grind-plate (also called a kick-plate). This is great if you're into trick-work, cuz it will help protect the bottom of your scoot. It fits underneath the deck, and attaches to the foot-brake and just behind the front wheel. You can get them in loads of different styles and colors. I have a silver one with a *Star Wars* emblem.

Trick-pegs

Trick-pegs can be a great addition for stunt-riding, too. You have to get specially made wheels that have a connection point for the pegs to slide into, but there should soon be scooter wheels ready-made with pegs attached. I've only seen a couple of people with them fitted so far, but they are totally fun to have because you can do a lot more tricks. Especially if you mount them on the front and back wheels!

Bag It!

The best accessory of all? This one you can have without making any changes to your scoot! It's a specially designed carry sack, so that you can sling the scooter over your shoulder when you're not using it. Most of the scooter-makers sell them, but it's pretty easy to make your own. Mine's light blue, like Qui-Gon's lightsaber! There are also special backpacks you can buy now that have an extended pocket to slide your scoot into. These are pretty cool if you ride your scoot to school – you can keep it separate from your books so they don't get messed up.

These tricks are a little harder than those you've already tried. Most can be done anywhere, as long as you have flat ground and some curbing. But for the ones toward the end of this chapter, you will need a mini-ramp. They come in all shapes and sizes and you can buy them in most skate shops.

Ramps vary a lot in height. The Streetstylers' advice is to start on a small one and work your way up. Landing a scoot – especially a two-wheeler – after a jump is NOT easy.

Again, the most important thing about riding your scooter – especially if you're going to try tricks – is to always wear the proper safety equipment. You'll be sorry if you don't. And before you try any of these harder tricks, make **sure** you have the easier stuff nailed first.

Grinds

Any time you Ollie up and slide along a surface using a part of your scoot other than the wheels, you are grinding. And it's music to the Streetstylers' ears! There's nothing like the sound of a scoot gliding along a curb, rail, step, or ledge. MMMMMMMM!!!!!!

Make sure you fit a grind-plate if you want to try this type of trick – otherwise you're gonna go through a lot of scoot decks!

DeckSlide

This is the most common type of grind, and the one you should learn first. It's a trick that will help you get the feel of how your scoot slides along different obstacles (curb, rail, wooden box, low-wall, whatever). It's also the safest way to test if an obstacle is slideable before you attack it with a more complicated trick!

Do The Trick

The Streetstylers' method is to cruise toward the obstacle at about 45°, then, when we get

to about 12 inches away, spring an Ollie. From that distance, you should be able to land with half the deck on and half off the obstacle.

Land facing straight up onto the sidewalk. Center your weight and let your momentum sliiiiiiiiiiiiiide you along.

The slide will last longer if you shift your weight back and forth on the scooter – this will help you keep your balance, too. When you hit the point where you're about to lose your balance cuz the scooter has slowed down so much (or you are running out of obstacle!), turn the scooter at least 45°. Not too much more though; you don't want the wheels to snag the obstacle cuz that will spill you. Then Ollie back off, making sure you get at least a 90° turn to be sure of a clean clearance.

If you don't find this totally addictive, the Streetstylers are gonna be truly amazed! In fact, we think that as soon as you master it, you'll want to try the **SlantedGrind**. To do the **SlantedGrind**, all you do differently is land the deck of your scoot on the curb or rail at a slight angle – something like 45°. It's a little more challenging cuz it's harder to maintain momentum this way. And remember that because the scoot is angled, you will probably need to twist it a little when you come to Ollie off.

You could also try the **SlantedGrind**

180°. This time, as you approach the curb, pull a 180° so that you land and grind facing backward! This move not only looks way cool, it's great if you need to make a quick getaway – you're already facing the path to freedom!

Rodeo 180°

This is a stunt you can perform standing still or on the move, and the idea is to spin your scooter through 180° using only the back wheel. To do this right, you have to use your body weight to spin the scooter, then try to shift your balance onto the back wheel so that the scoot's front end stays up throughout the turn.

Do The Trick

Place your right foot over the brake and back wheel, then slide your left foot down to nestle against it. Next, gripping the handlebar firmly in your left hand, raise your right hand away from your body – like a rodeo rider! OK, you might *feel* a little stupid, but it's the only way you will be able to balance during the trick.

Now that you're in position, spin your body quickly so it moves around and away from the scoot. As long as you keep a good grip on the handlebars, they should turn with you. Meanwhile, the momentum of your turn should carry the scoot through a half-circle – as long as you can stay balanced on that back wheel (the difficult part!). Once you've spun, slide your foot back down the deck and rebalance on two wheels.

If you can do this move while surfing along, the Streetstylers will be seriously impressed! But don't get too cocky. As soon as you have the 180° in the bag, you should try the . . .

Rodeo 360°

To pocket this stunt, you do the same moves as with a 180°, but cuz you are going twice as far, you will need to spin your body *much* faster and be even *more* carefully balanced.

This is one of the Streetstylers' all-time favorite tricks. If you can pull it off in motion (which requires a *lot* of speed), the Rodeo 360° looks absolutely awesome.

X-Up

This trick is based on an old BMX classic. It's a simple idea that works just as well on flat ground as in a pipe at a skate park. You get some air, then turn the scooter's handlebars through 180° *and* back again before landing. No worries!

Do The Trick

First, glide up to a good cruising speed and get ready to Ollie. As soon as you leave the ground, pull the right handlebar upward, and push the left downward. You'll know when you've pushed the front wheel through 180° because your arms will cross (forming an X-shape). As soon as that happens, twist the bars back to the starting position ready to land in the same way you would for a normal Ollie.

This stunt is a lot trickier than it sounds. If

you have trouble getting it dialed, don't worry. It took the Streetstylers weeks to get it right. And there *is* an easier way: The T-Up. All you do is grip the handlebars at their central point, and twist from there. You still get a 180°, and it's just a tiny bit less awesome . . .

If you do get to grips with a full-on X-Up, try landing with your arms still crossed. That's so tough it might even earn a little respect from Chloe.

Yeah, if you can do it with both feet off the board, too!

Nose Wheelie

This is another trick that comes to scooting from the world of BMX-ing. Like the X-Up, it sounds simple and looks great, but can be tricky to pull off. It might seem like the reverse of the Ollie Manual, but it's definitely harder!

If you have one of the newest model scoots with a built-in front brake, then this is your lucky day. You should be able to per-form this one pretty easily – just lock that brake and lean into it. For the rest of us, it's gonna take a lot of practice, because we will be relying totally on balance.

A good tip for getting this move together is to practice on grass. That way the front wheel sinks into the ground slightly and you can start to get a feel for where to position your body to keep from falling.

Do The Trick

First, you need to get a good grip on the handlebars, then slide your body weight toward the front of the scooter. It might help you to rest your side against the handlebars to help maintain balance. That won't win you many prizes for technique, but it'll get the trick done.

As your weight moves down the scoot, you will feel the back wheel begin to rise. The trick is to find the point where you are balanced with the back end quite high off the ground, but that you haven't slid too far forward so that the scoot would shoot out from under you.

This is the kind of trick that doesn't look that impressive to people who don't ride scooters, so you should only pop it when you are with those in the know. They will see how much you've sweated to get it right and give you the credit you deserve. Especially if you start hopping on that front wheel, too!!

TailWhip

A TailWhip (sometimes called a PopTail-ShoveIt) is just about the trickiest stunt you can pull without ramps or pipes. It is also one of the few tricks that can't be attempted on a skateboard, bike, or in-lines.

Yep – TailWhips are unique to scooter riders! And they are definitely worth all the effort (and bruises!) of learning. The TailWhip is amazing to watch and will get you *maximum* respect from your fellow riders!

The basic idea is to Ollie, then spin the scoot's deck right out from under you and through 360° while your body is still airborne. You touch down on the deck again just as it completes its spin. Simple, right?!!!

Well . . . Maybe not. Which is why it's a cool idea to learn the Semi-TailWhip first. For this stunt, the Streetstylers say it's OK for your feet to touch the ground! And, like the other complicated tricks, you should try this one on the spot before attempting it in motion – unless you live for road rash! Landing on a spinning deck is HARD!

Ollie | Spin that deck! | Back on deck!

Do The Trick

Keeping your right foot on the scooter, place your left on the ground so that it's parallel to the front wheel. This foot will act as your pivot. Just as you plant it, flick the tail of the scoot with your right foot so that it spins away real fast in a counterclockwise direction.

Keep a tight grip on the handlebars so they don't turn with the rest of the scoot, and the deck should shoot right around in front of you, spinning back toward your left side. As it completes its circuit, jump your left leg back up and onto the board – and try to make a steady landing!

 **Once you've got it down – and it does take time – try and pull it off in motion. The trick here is getting a good swift gliding speed, and kicking the board out fast enough that it comes back around before your legs are stretched all over the sidewalk!! Get that in the bag and you are ready to try the full TailWhip!**

Because you don't touch the ground at all with a full TailWhip it can seem almost impossible to perform. The Streetstylers say you can solve this by breaking the stunt down into sections. When you've got each part down, try to execute them together.

Do The Trick

Start off by practicing flicking the deck around with your feet. Then practice the landing – which shouldn't be too hard if you can already do the Semi-TailWhip.

To do the full trick, bend your legs as if you were going to Ollie. As you spring up, flick your feet out to either the right or left to make the deck spin away from under you. Hold the handlebars tight, otherwise the scooter will spin off down the street. If you've timed it right, the scooter's deck should spin through 180° just as you reach the top point of your jump, completing its circuit just as your feet come down. Then all you have to do is hit the deck and land like you would for an Ollie.

Ramp Jumps

If you want to ramp jump on a scooter, there's one thing you need a lot of: SPEED! You should place your ramp at the bottom of a steep hill, or use a launch ramp to build up enough momentum. (If you live somewhere flat, check to see if your skate park has ramp facilities before you think about buying two ramps!!). Don't attempt ramp tricks unless you are sure of a lot of speed. It's just too dangerous. You'll either tip right off the end of your ramp, or fade mid-jump and end up smeared all across the floor. So, before you try the ramp, do a few test runs alongside it to make sure you go a good distance.

One Footer

This is the best one to learn first as it's all about jumping and landing with confidence, and getting the feel of ramp work in preparation for harder stunts. You don't even have to jump that high with One Footers. And no one will point and laugh if your leg doesn't make it back onto the deck before you land. As long as you get from the start of the jump to the end in one piece, you're a success!

Do The Trick

To pull it off, race toward the ramp at a good speed (you will soon get to know what kind of pace you need to do good jumps) and clear the ramp. When you reach the highest point of your leap, kick out one of your feet to the left- or right-hand side. (It MUST be to the side, otherwise you will unbalance and wipe out HUGELY.) Hold your foot out for as long as you comfortably can, then try to bring it back to the deck before you land.

The first time you try this, you'll probably only manage a superfast little flick-kick, and it'll seem impossible to do any more. But as you get used to the feel of being in the air with only one foot on the deck you will be able to hold it out there longer and longer. Then you can try the . . .

Can-Can

This trick is named after a crazy dance invented in France cuz it uses the same leg movements. You don't have to wear a frilly dress to do it (unless you really want to!). The trick can be performed in several different ways, but the one you'll see tricksters attempting most often is called the One-Footed Can-Can.

Do The Trick

To get it dialed, head for the ramp at a good jumping speed. As you take the jump, do the smallest of One Footers off to the side. It doesn't really need to be a kick, just enough movement for your foot to leave the deck. Then bring your foot across the deck and kick it out very slightly to the other side (strangely, it's not as hard as it sounds!). To complete the move, kick back to the original position and bring your foot to rest on the deck again as you land.

For your first few attempts, you probably won't manage to complete the move, but you'll be freaked by how much you can move your legs in the short time you're in the air! Once you've realized that, the Streetstylers know you'll be trying all kinds of crazy variations.

One Hander

Trying to take a hand off the handlebars mid-jump is harder than lifting a foot in midair. Probably because you *think* you are gonna accidentally twist the steering column – even if you *know* you won't! And once you've done a few jumps, you'll know that it can be very bad when that happens.

Do The Trick

Head toward the ramp at your normal, comfortable jumping speed. Before you launch into the air, decide which hand you are going to lift clear of the grip. It's probably best to keep your stronger hand on the handlebars for the first few tries. You won't be quite so nervous about letting your weaker hand do the flapping around!

Just before you reach the highest point in your jump, release the handlebars. The first time you try it, it's a good idea to just relax your hold on the grip, but keep your hand resting on it. It'll give you more confidence for your next run. As you land, close your hand back around the grip.

It'll probably take you quite a few tries to become comfortable with even moving your hand a tiny bit away from the handlebars, but with enough practice you will be moving it a lot – maybe even waving to your fans down on the ground!!

No Footer

If you like your tricks burly, this is one for you! You need to be very confident with all the other ramp moves before you even think about attempting the No Footer.

Do The Trick

Cruise up the ramp at your normal jumping speed and launch out. At the highest point of your jump, pull both your feet off the deck and kick them out to the sides. You need to be perfectly balanced to do this, and you must be sure that your steering column is attached properly, cuz it's gonna be taking all your weight.

As with the One Footer and the Can-Can, your kicks don't have to be huge – you will be able to go bigger the more you practice. You MUST get both feet back onto the board before you land though. The Streetstylers don't want to think about what will happen to your knees otherwise. YEEEOOOOUU-UCHHH!!!

And that's it. Once you've learned all these, you should throw away your scoot, cuz there's nothing left to learn. **JUST KIDDING!**

There are *hundreds* more stunts and variations of stunts you can do on your scooter, and we're gonna show you a whole load more of them in chapter eleven. So, get out there and practice, practice, practice. And repeat after the Streetstylers: I can do this trick. I CAN do this trick. I CAN DO THIS TRICK!!!

If you've got a scooter problem, and if no one else can help, and if you can find him, maybe you should ask the Dek Doktor.

Yeah, maybe you should.

Let's take a look through his bulging mail-bag:

I just bought a Kickboard and it's really wobbly. Is something wrong with the wheels?

Troy (Seattle)

Could be. But ride it a few times anyhow – it may be the rider, not the scooter.

Hi Dok! I have an old Micro that used to be my bro's. When I Ollie, it sounds like it's gonna break. Should I get a new one?

Burly Paul (Houston)

Tricky one. It takes a lot to break a scoot, but the older ones do weaken in the end – especially around the rear axle. Keep on using it. If all you're doing is Ollies, the worst that'll happen is a break. Then you should retire the scoot with full honors! Don't use it for more than that though. No point in taking stupid chances! Get a new scooter with suspension for tougher tricks.

Dok,
The Streetstylers say when you wheelie on your front wheel it's a Nose Wheelie. I always thought it was a Hang Ten. Who's right?

Krazy Rob (Glasgow)

 **Both of you. Tricks have lots of different names. It mostly depends on where you come from. Some tricks change their names because they become recognized as a particular scoot-head's trademark. Maybe one day the Nose Wheelie will be called Krazy's Nose!**

Dear Dek Doktor,
My brake squeaks really bad on hills. How do I stop this?

Marisa (New York)

 **Check that the brake and the wheel are both free of grit and dirt, and make sure the wheel is tightened properly. If the wheel runs straight and free of dirt, you shouldn't have a squeak problem.**

Dek,
I know this guy with really ugly hair. It's really short on the front and sides, but really long in the back. Is this a mullet?

KT-90 (London)

Yes!

Dear Doktor,
If I make changes to my scooter and then it gets broken, will the manufacturer still replace it?

Jon (Denmark)

 **That totally depends on the changes you make. If you use products that your scoot-maker officially endorses, then they will replace the scooter if it breaks due to a design or build fault. But if you make any other modifications – even a new paint job! – you might be canceling your warranty.**

Hi! I just got a scooter and I want to put different-colored wheels and ABEC bearings on, but I can't get the old wheels off. What do I do?

Corsten (Munich)

It can be hard to find the right-sized Allen wrench to remove your wheels. If you tried already with one that wasn't the right size, you may have stripped the head. Take your scooter to a skate shop and let the pros sort it out! One good thing – once you replace the wheels, you will get the right size Allen wrench, cuz most packs come with one included.

Dok,
I saw some guy with these weird, curved side-plates screwed onto his deck. What are they for?

Carla (Maine)

Some people have started widening their decks with "wings." It's a simple modification that most skate shops can do for you. Wings help stabilize the scooter, making tricks easier because they leave more room for your feet.

Dek,
What's the quickest and easiest way to make my Micro faster?

Jen (Illinois)

Try changing your wheels. 110 mm ones should fit just as well as those your scoot came with, and that extra 10mm makes a real difference to your gliding speed.

Dear Dr.,
My mom says I can't have a scooter because they are too dangerous. She says thousands of kids have cut off their fingers trying to unfold their scooters. Is she right?

Matt (Oxford)

117

It's true that people get hurt riding scoots. But your mom should chill a little – as long as you are wearing the right safety gear. However, some scooters have been recalled as they have sharp edges on the steering column that you only see when you are folding your scooter. The Dok recomends sanding any sharp edges as soon as you get your scoot. Most scooters already have this done, but checking hurts a lot less than a severed fingertip!

You Got the Skills to Pay the Bills! 11

This section is for those of you who want to follow in the footsteps of the pros.

You won't find any easy stunts on these pages. They're called tricks cuz they are TRICKY. But, if you put in the practice, the Streetstylers know you will get 'em dialed. There are *not* a lot of scoot-riders out there who can pull off all these big-time crowd pleasers. But never, ever try them unless you are totally comfortable with the earlier tricks and you are somewhere with adult supervision.

TECH-TALK!

Concave = A tranny that arcs inward.
Convex = A tranny that arcs outward.
Coping = Any grindable and slideable material attached to an obstacle to make grinds and slides easier. Most commonly found at the top end of trannys such as half-pipes.

Half-Pipe = A specially made ramp with concave transitions at each end.
Transition = (Tranny) = Any surface for skating that isn't totally horizontal or vertical – anything from the slightest dip or hump to a fully concave pipe.

Most of these stunts can be done anywhere. But for a few, you need to visit a skate park and get yourself onto a transition. If you're up for giving that a try, choose a park where the equipment is in good shape, there is some kind of supervision, and you have access to a phone. Scoot injuries in skate parks are rare, but they can happen. So it's good that you're wearing all your safeties, right? Right! Then let's BURNNNNNNNNNN!!!

Drop In

This is a little move for making a stylish entry into a concave transition like a half-pipe. It's simple but scary, cuz you are basically hurling yourself and your scoot out off a precipice! If you've not tried this kind of transition before, you should ride it a few times without doing stunts to get used to the weird feeling.

Done that? Cool. Let's Drop Innnnn!!!

Do The Trick

Position the scooter so that its front third is right out over the coping. Keep your back foot onboard – and on the brake – to prevent the scooter from tipping into the pipe too soon. Take a good deep breath (!)

step your other foot forward onto the deck, and grab the handlebars, crouching low over the scoot, so it and your body will tilt down into the transition together.

Make sure you lean a long way forward and are *determined* to complete the trick. If you hesitate or panic, the deck can shoot out from under you – even if you're gripping the handlebars firmly. You really don't want that to happen. No sir.

But don't lean *too* far. You'll end up plunging down the transition ahead of your scooter – probably collecting the handlebars in your gut along the way! You don't want that to happen, either.

The bad news is . . . Unless you're really lucky, you will only know the right distance to lean by wiping out a few times. Well, hey . . . The Streetstylers never told you these moves would be easy!

Rock 'n' Roll

To complete this trick you first need to have enough speed to reach the coping at the top of the transition. You can kick back and forth in the pipe to build up that kind of speed, or use the momentum you already have from another trick like the Drop In.

Do The Trick

When your scooter reaches the coping, get your front wheel and part of the deck over the edge. Then quickly lean in with your front foot so you are rocking back and forth, balanced on the coping. And that's the easy part! Now you have to switch your weight into an Ollie-ing position and perform a 180°. The trick here is clearing the coping with your wheels as you turn. Otherwise you'll make a big scootery mess all the way down the pipe! If you do manage the turn, slip straight into the Drop In move and scoot back down the transition ready to receive the Streetstyler Medal of Maximum Respect!!!

50-50

For this move you need to combine good pipe-work with grinding skills you've already learned. Before you try it, you need to get to grips with stalling your scoot up on the coping. That way you can get your head around how to balance on the lip of the tranny – an essential part of pulling off a good grind.

Do The Trick

Work up some speed so that you can race head-on to the top of the transition. As your front wheel clears the coping, flick the back end of the scoot into an angled slide so that it spins through 90°. Then try to balance on the lip of the tranny without toppling. (The first few times you will probably have to put your foot down for support.) When you have this dialed, you can try for the grind.

Head up that transition with some serious speed. Make sure you are at an angle, too – otherwise you'll fly straight out of the pipe! As your front wheel clears the lip of the tranny, spin the back end of the scoot almost as far as you would to stall, but not enough that the back wheel clears the coping. Then lean your weight forward and toward the coping, and let your momentum glide you along in a SERIOUS grinding action! Oh, and don't forget to spin into a Drop In before you run out of pipe!

Grabs

You're doing one of these any time you reach down and grasp your deck while in the air. But guess what . . . ? Grabs are *hard* on a scooter! The "easiest" way to do them is to crouch low and reach for the deck-plate just in front of your front foot. Be careful of the deck wheel – the Streetstylers don't want to see anyone get their fingers smashed! Try your first grabs when you're Ollie-ing on flat ground. When you get used to the action, give it a try on a tranny.

Do The Trick

Take it easy and go up the slope at only a slight angle. If you try to carve into it big style, all you'll end up doing is sailing to the ground while your scoot flies off over the coping. So . . . aim small till you've got control!

As you near the top of the curve, you should begin to reach for the scoot's deck so that when your front wheel clears the coping, your hand will be closing for the grab. Then as your back wheel hits the coping, put the slightest pressure on your back foot. This will help bring the deck into your hand, as well as send you in the right direction – UP!

This is The Streetstylers Signing Off!

The world of scooters is movin' on up, changing, and transforming all the time. The Streetstylers may have said our piece, but we know there will be a million and one more things to say a few months from now – and you will be a part of it! Already we heard rumors of a new generation of scooters that are gonna blow your minds.

We've still got a couple of spaces in our posse – if we can find anyone good enough to fill them. So we're gonna be out there, watching all you guys. Practice enough, and you could be riding with us. Shoulder to shoulder.

Peace . . .